7-30

20,000 LEAGUES UNDER THE SEA

20,000 LEAGUES UNDER THE SEA

By Jules Verne

Adapted by Lillian Nordlicht
Illustrated by Steve Butz

Raintree Publishers • Milwaukee • Toronto • Melbourne • London

Copyright © 1980, Raintree Publishers Inc.

All rights reserved. No part of this book may be
reproduced or utilized in any form or by any means,
electronic or mechanical, including photocopying,
recording, or by any information storage and retrieval
system, without permission in writing from the Publisher.
Inquiries should be addressed to Raintree Publishers Inc.,
205 West Highland Avenue, Milwaukee, Wisconsin 53203.

Library of Congress Number: 79-23887

1 2 3 4 5 6 7 8 9 0 84 83 82 81 80

Printed in the United States of America.

Library of Congress Cataloging in Publication Data

Nordlicht, Lillian.
  20,000 leagues under the sea.

  SUMMARY: An adaptation of the 19th-century science
fiction tale of an electric submarine, its eccentric
captain, and undersea world which anticipated many of
the scientific achievements of the 20th century.
  [1. Sea stories.   2.   Submarines — Fiction.
3. Science fiction] I. Butz, Steve. II. Verne,
Jules, 1828-1905.   Vingt mille lieues sous les mers.
III. Title.
PZ7.N77547Tw   [Fic]   79-23887
ISBN 0-8172-1652-9 lib. bdg.

CONTENTS

I FORM MY RESOLUTION

1

My name is Professor Aronnax, and I will always remember the year 1867, in which events took place that changed the course of my life.

For some time, a strange creature had been attacking vessels off the coast of Australia. Long and spindle-shaped, it had amazing speed, and it could blow a column of water one hundred and fifty feet into the air. It could and did leave a large hole in the bottom of both wooden and steel ships.

At first, it was thought by seafaring men to be a reef. But no such reef appeared on any charted maps. Then it was thought to be a whale. But no one had ever seen a whale that size.

That this gigantic creature existed, no one denied. There were too many unexplained shipwrecks, and too many damaged ships were pulling into drydock for repairs.

"Rid the seas of this danger!" the public demanded. "Relieve us of this menace!"

I had just arrived in New York from some scientific research in Nebraska for the Museum of Natural History in Paris. I was leaving for France with my scientific treasures in May. While I was preparing for my journey home, the vessel *Scotia* was attacked by something of enormous strength, and her bottom steel plates, which were 1⅜ inches thick, were pierced.

This mystery puzzled me. Because I had written books about underseas life, the *New York Herald* asked me for my opinion.

"It must be a gigantic narwhal," I said. "A sea-unicorn of colossal size armed with a spur."

Three hours before my boat sailed from the Brooklyn dock I received a letter. It read:

To M. Aronnax, Professor in the Museum of Paris,
Fifth Avenue Hotel, New York.

Sir, If you will consent to join the *Abraham Lincoln* in this expedition, the Government of the United States will with pleasure see France represented in the enterprise. Commander Farragut has a cabin at your disposal.

Very cordially yours,
J. B. Hobson,
Secretary of Marine

Although I was tired, and longed to see my country and my friends, I accepted without hesitation. Nothing could have kept me away.

Conseil was my servant. He was a true, devoted Flemish boy who had been with me for the last ten years.

"Conseil," I called. "Make preparations. We leave in two hours. We go aboard the *Abraham Lincoln* in search of the monster—the famous narwhal. We are going to purge it from the seas."

"And your collections, sir?" asked Conseil.

"They will be forwarded to France by the hotel."

In no time at all, we were packed, and our luggage was transported to the deck of the *Abraham Lincoln*.

There a good-looking officer held out his hand. "You are welcome, Professor, your cabin is ready for you," said Commander Farragut.

While Conseil stowed our trunks away, I watched Commander Farragut order the last moorings cast off. Eight bells struck. We lost sight of lights. We were off in the dark waters of the Atlantic.

No ship was better built, armed and equipped than the *Abraham Lincoln*, and no ship had a better commander.

Captain Farragut had sworn to rid the seas of the monster. He offered a sum of two thousand dollars to the first person who spotted the creature.

All eyes watched the sea, including my own. On board was the prince of harpooners, Ned Land, who had no equal in this dangerous occupation. He was a Canadian, about forty years old and strongly built. He was a quiet man, but violent when contradicted.

Little by little I drew him out, and we took a strong liking to each other. One day I led the conversation around to our search.

"Why are you doubtful it is a whale we are following?" said I.

"As a whaler, I harpooned many, but not one was ever able to scratch the iron plates of a steamer," replied Ned.

"How about a mass hurling itself with the speed of an express train against the hull of a ship?"

"Perhaps," replied the Canadian. "But if such creatures exist, they must be as strong as you say."

The voyage was good. So was the weather. But there was no sign of the monster even though every point of the American and Japanese coast was explored.

The sailors could not hide their disappointment and they became bored. It showed in their work and attitude.

"Give me three days," requested Captain Farragut. "If the monster does not appear, the *Abraham Lincoln* will make for home."

The promise rallied the ship's crew. Nothing happened for two days. Then on the night of the 4th of November, a voice was heard. It was the voice of Ned Land shouting—

"Look out there! The very thing we are looking for—on our weather beam!"

My heart beat as if it would break as the monster emerged with a light that lit the sea around it.

"That brightness is of an electrical nature," I said. "And it is heading right for us!"

"Reverse the engines," cried Captain Farragut.

The *Abraham Lincoln* fled, and did not attack.

"What we are facing is a gigantic narwhal, and an electric one. It must be the most terrible animal created. I must be on my guard and not risk my ship in this darkness. Daylight, and the scene will change," said Captain Farragut.

At six o'clock, day began to break. The time for the struggle had arrived.

The *Abraham Lincoln* went straight at the animal, but this time the animal fled. We could not catch up with it. What a pursuit! Several times the animal let us gain upon it. But just as Ned Land was going to strike, it stole away.

A cry of fury rose from everyone!

At noon, we were no further advanced than at eight o'clock in the morning.

A gun was loaded, and a shot fired. The bullet hit the animal, but not fatally, and the chase began again.

I wished the beast would exhaust itself. But hours passed without it showing any signs of exhaustion. Then at ten o'clock at night, the narwhal seemed tired with its day's work.

"Now is the time to take advantage," said Captain Farragut. He gave his orders. The frigate approached noiselessly and stopped at two cables' lengths from the motionless animal.

Ned Land threw his terrible harpoon, and a loud sound was heard as it struck a hard body. Suddenly the electric light went out, and two enormous waterspouts rushed like a flood over the bridge of the frigate.

Before I could stop myself, I was thrown over the rail, and I fell into the sea.

THE NAUTILUS

2

The fall stunned me. I am a good swimmer, though, and two strokes brought me to the surface. Had anyone seen me disappear? Would the captain put out a boat?

Although it was dark, I caught a glimpse of a black mass disappearing in the distance. It was the ship! I was lost.

"Help! Help!" I shouted in desperation.

My clothes were heavy. They were dragging me down. Suddenly a strong hand grasped me.

"If master would be so good as to lean on my shoulder, master would swim with much greater ease."

"Is it you?" said I as I seized Conseil's arm. "You?"

"Myself," answered Conseil, "and waiting master's orders."

"Did that shock throw you into the sea?" I asked.

"No, but being in my master's service, I followed him." He seemed to think that this was perfectly natural.

"And the frigate?"

"The screw and rudder were broken by the monster's teeth."

"Then we are lost!"

"Not yet," calmly answered Conseil. "We still have several hours. One can do a great deal."

We swam next to each other for hours. A very calm sea was in our favor. But near one o'clock in the morning, I had a violent cramp in my legs. Conseil held me up in the water.

"Leave me!" I said to Conseil.

"Leave my master? Never!" he replied. "I would drown first."

Just then the moon lit up the sea. I saw the frigate five miles away from us.

"Help! Help!" cried Conseil.

A human voice answered ours! But I scarcely heard it because I was so exhausted—I sank!

A hard body struck me, and I clung to it. I was drawn up, and fainted. When I came to, I saw a face I immediately recognized.

"Ned!" I cried. "Were you thrown into the sea by the shock of the frigate?"

"Yes, Professor, but I was able to find footing upon our gigantic narwhal."

"Explain yourself, Ned!"

"Our beast is made of iron."

Sure enough, the blackish back that held me was without scales. I gave it a blow which produced a metallic sound. There was no doubt about it. We were lying on the back of a sort of submarine boat! A fish of steel!

"As long as it sails on the surface, we are safe," said Ned Land. "But I would not give two straws for our lives if it takes a fancy to dive." He kicked the plate. "Open! Open! You miserable creature!"

A noise came from inside the boat. One iron plate moved aside. A man appeared and disappeared. Moments later, eight strong men with masked faces drew us down into their machine. At the bottom of the ladder a door opened and shut after us.

We were alone.

"Happily, I still have my bowie-knife, and I can see well enough to use it," cried Ned Land. "The first of these pirates who lays a hand on me—"

Our prison suddenly lit up with the same electric light that had played around the submarine boat. Two men appeared.

One had the look of men who came from Southern

France. The other had the most admirable face I had ever seen. His black eyes were cold and calm. His deep breathing showed great power of lungs and energy. He was tall, had a large forehead, straight nose, and beautiful teeth. He spoke to his companion in an unknown tongue.

I told of our adventures in good French. Both men listened, but did not seem to understand me. Ned tried English, Conseil German, and I tried to remember my Latin. They did not answer.

The two strangers left, and Ned Land was furious. "My opinion is formed. They are rascals. Otherwise they would have answered us. We shall die of hunger in this iron cage!"

As he said these words, the door opened. A steward carrying dry clothes entered. He laid three settings on the table. Words were engraved on the silverware.

MOBILIS IN MOBILI

N

Moving in the moving element! A good motto for this ship. N was doubtless the initial of its commander.

The food was excellent. So was the service. While we were eating, thoughts crowded my brain. Where were we? What strange power carried us on?

As soon as our appetites were satisfied, I fell into a deep sleep. But before I did, I felt the ship sinking down to the lowest beds of the sea.

When I woke my mind was clear. But the air was heavy and hurt my lungs.

Suddenly pure air entered the room.

Ned and Conseil woke at the same time. "There seems to be a sea breeze," said Ned.

"Right," I answered. "The submarine was taking a breath."

We were all very hungry. But hours went by before the door opened. When at last it did, Ned Land seized the steward by the throat.

"Release him!" ordered a voice in French. "I am Captain

Nemo, commander of the vessel *Nautilus*." The large man from the previous day appeared. Ned Land complied.

"I delayed this second visit because I wished to think about what to do with you. Your ship attacked me and you are my prisoners of war. If I choose, I could place you on deck, sink beneath the waters, and forget you ever existed."

"That would be the act of a savage," I said.

"I am not a civilized man," said the commander quickly. "Never refer to the laws of society. However, I have decided to allow you to remain aboard this vessel."

"Never to see our country, our friends, our relatives again?" I asked.

"Yes, sir."

"I will never give my word not to try to escape!" cried Ned Land.

"I did not ask for your word," said Captain Nemo coldly. "Breakfast is ready. Permit me to lead the way."

I sat next to Captain Nemo. "All of our food comes from the sea," he told me. "It is wholesome and nourishing. My crew and I are never ill."

When we finished, "Now, Professor," he said, "if you wish to go over the *Nautilus,* I am at your service."

There were over twelve thousand books in the library. In the museum I saw works of great value by old masters. Under glass cases were the most precious shells and productions of the sea. Pearls of great value reflected the electric light in sparks of fire.

"But it is the *Nautilus* that excites my curiousity the most," I confessed. "I see instruments I do not know."

"I will gladly explain them. The same instruments are in my room which is next to yours," said the commander. His room was sparse and plain while mine was elegant. I listened closely.

"The barometer indicates the weather, and the hygrometer the dryness of the atmosphere. The storm glass announces the approach of storms, and the compass guides our course. These other instruments give us our latitude and longitude. The electricity which powers us is taken from the sea."

"But the sea does not give you the air you breathe?" I asked.

"It is not necessary. I can come to the surface for air when I please. Now follow me."

In the center of the boat was an iron ladder. "Where does it lead to?" I asked.

"It leads to a small boat which I use for fishing and pleasure."

"How do you get back on board?"

"There is an electric cord that connects us. I signal and the *Nautilus* comes and gets me."

I was astonished by these marvels and asked many questions. Captain Nemo answered them without hesitation. "Since you may never leave this submarine, I will hold nothing back."

Finally, "Ah, Captain Nemo, your *Nautilus* is a marvelous boat," I said. "One last question."

"Ask it, Professor."

"You are rich?"

"I could, sir, without missing it, pay the national debt of France."

I stared at the man who spoke thus. Was he telling me the truth? The future would decide that.

He left me, and I was examining the map of the currents of the Pacific Ocean by myself, when Ned and Conseil appeared.

"Can you tell me how many men are on board?" asked Ned Land.

"I cannot answer you, and you had better abandon all idea of escape. Many people would accept the situation if only to move among such wonders."

"But we are in an iron prison!" exclaimed the harpooner, when suddenly the room went dark.

Two panels opened and two crystal plates, vividly lit up,

separated us from the sea. We could see a mile around the *Nautilus!* The water shimmered around us. We passed through schools of gray and white triggerfish, rays that moved like sheets in the wind, and long, spiny sea eels. What a spectacle! For two hours we enjoyed this immense aquarium. Then the iron panels closed and Ned and Conseil returned to their cabins.

I passed the evening reading, writing, and thinking. Then sleep overpowered me, and I slept soundly.

THE STRAITS OF TORRES

3

In the days that followed, we enjoyed perfect liberty, but Ned Land was always thinking of escape. There was no sign of Captain Nemo.

Then one day, we received an invitation to a hunting party in the undersea forests of Crespo. Captain Nemo and some of his crew helped us into rubber diving suits and lead shoes. Copper helmets containing compressed air were strapped to our backs. Lamps were issued along with guns firing special electric bullets that could kill instantly.

"But how shall we gain the bottom of the sea?" I asked.

"You shall see."

We were pushed into a small water-tight room which began to fill with water. When it was full, a door on the side of the *Nautilus* opened. Our feet trod the bottom of the sea!

All around us were undersea gardens, strange fish, shells and rocks. Large tree plants reached for the rays of the sun. We walked for hours. Then tired, we halted and slept. When I awoke, I found a monstrous sea-spider watching me, ready to spring. Captain Nemo hit it with his gun. Further along he shot a magnificent sea-otter, and fired at a large albatross that could be seen flying above the water. We walked two more hours, then turned back.

The outer door of the *Nautilus* was open. After we entered, Captain Nemo closed it. Then he pressed a knob and the water drained out of the small room.

The next morning, we surfaced to renew our supply of oxygen. I was on the platform when Captain Nemo appeared.

"Is not this ocean gifted?" he said. "In it there is no lack of excellent food. I can imagine nautical towns, submarine houses, independent cities. Yet who know whether some cruel ruler—." He changed the subject.

I seldom saw him during the weeks that followed. But the books in the library, the writing of my memoirs, and the sight of the beautiful waters in the windows of the saloon took up all of my time. I was never bored. I also saw many hulls of shipwrecked vessels rotting in the depths of the ocean. They were a sad and sorry sight.

The *Nautilus* traveled with great speed. One day Captain Nemo informed me he planned to get to the Indian Ocean by the Torres Straits. Rocks made navigation dangerous. As we approached the island of Gilboa, we ran aground on a coral reef.

"I think it is time to part company with Captain Nemo for a while," said Ned Land.

"I agree," said Conseil. "Could master get permission to put us on land?"

To my great surprise, Captain Nemo gave the permission I asked for.

Armed with guns and hatchets, we got off the *Nautilus*.

It took little time to row to the island. While we were gathering fruits and nuts, "Suppose we never return to the ship?" said Ned Land.

A stone fell at our feet.

"Savages!" I cried as a man, ten yards from me, aimed his sling. As we headed for the boat, stones and arrows fell thickly around us.

When we were on board, I found Captain Nemo at his organ.

"Did you have a good hunt?" he asked.

"Unfortunately, we ran into a group of savages."

"You are astonished at finding savages on a strange island?" he asked with a smile.

The natives paddled out to the *Nautilus* and spent the night uttering deafening cries.

"Will they board us when we come up for air?" I asked Captain Nemo the next morning.

"Let them come," he replied.

When the port lids were pulled down, twenty native faces appeared. The first native touched the stair rail and felt a powerful shock. The outside of the boat had been electrified. Terrified, he fled. His companions met the same fate.

The *Nautilus,* raised by the tide, quit her coral reef. Then we passed safely through the Straits of Torres.

On the 28th of February, we received another invitation from Captain Nemo.

"The island of Ceylon is noted for its pearl fisheries. Would you like to visit one of them and see the fishermen at work?"

"Certainly," I replied.

"Is pearl-fishing dangerous?" asked Conseil.

"Not if precautions are taken," answered Captain Nemo. "By the way," he said to Ned Land, "are you afraid of sharks?"

"I!" replied the Canadian, "a harpooner by profession? My trade is to make light of them."

Early the next morning, Captain Nemo, four crewmen, Ned Land, Conseil and myself took off in the small boat to Minaar Island, where anchor was dropped. The crewmen helped us into our heavy sea-dress.

"But we will carry no electric light," said Captain Nemo. "It might attract some of the dangerous fish that live in these waters."

For protection, we each carried a strong knife. Ned Land had his large harpoon. The sun's rays lit up the ocean floor as we followed Captain Nemo into the water.

Ned Land was filling a net with some of the finest pearls at the oyster-banks, when Captain Nemo motioned for us to hide behind a rock. An Indian diver had come to pick oysters.

Suddenly, a gigantic shadow appeared above him, and

the diver tried to return to the surface. But an enormous shark hit him with its tail, and prepared to cut him in two with its sharp teeth.

Captain Nemo rose. Dagger in hand, he walked straight to the monster and buried his knife in its side. Then a terrible fight took place. Hard as he tried, Captain Nemo was unable to give a decisive blow, and he fell to earth exhausted. The shark's jaws opened wide.

Harpoon in hand, Ned Land quickly rushed towards the shark and pierced its heart.

Captain Nemo's first concern was to bring the Indian back to life upon the surface. He also placed a bag of pearls in the fisherman's trembling hands.

When we were back in the small boat, and rid of our copper helmets, he said "Thank you, Master Land."

"I was repaying a debt, Captain," replied Ned Land. "I owed you that."

A ghastly smile passed across the Captain's lips, and that was all.

On our way back to the Nautilus, we saw the shark's dead body floating by. It had an enormous mouth and was more than twenty-five feet long. While we were watching, a dozen more sharks began to devour the body and fight with one another for the pieces.

When we were back on board the Nautilus, I thought about the incredible courage of Captain Nemo, and his concern for another human being. Whatever he might say, this strange man had not yet succeeded in entirely crushing his heart.

When I said this to him, he answered in a slightly moved tone—

"That Indian, sir, lives in the land of the oppressed; and I belong, to my last breath, to that country!"

THE SOURCE OF MILLIONS

4

On the 12th of February, we were in the Mediterranean.

"Good," said Ned Land. "Let us talk. Before Captain Nemo drags us to the bottom of the Polar Seas, or leads us into Oceania, I want to leave the *Nautilus*."

"Are you tired of being on board? Are you sorry destiny has thrown us into Captain Nemo's hands?" I asked.

"Truthfully, I am glad to have made the trip. But now let us have done with it."

"Agreed! But our first attempt must succeed. If it fails, Captain Nemo will never forgive us. What is your plan?" I asked.

"When the *Nautilus* is near enough to some European coast, under the cover of darkness we will try to swim to shore."

Ned Land kept watching for a favorable opportunity to present itself, but the *Nautilus* kept far from the coast. Did Captain Nemo suspect anything, I wondered?

While we were waiting, I spent hours studying the fish passing before my eyes. One day, a diver carrying a leather purse in his belt appeared suddenly.

"A man is shipwrecked! He must be saved!" I cried to Captain Nemo.

To my great amazement, Captain Nemo signaled to the man, who rose to the surface and did not appear again.

"You know him?" I asked.

"Why not, Professor Aronnax?" he answered, opening a chest of iron that held a great many ingots of gold. Where did they come from, I wondered? And what was he going to do with them?

Captain Nemo fastened the chest securely. He wrote an address on the lid, then pressed a wire summoning four members of the crew. They hoisted the chest up the iron staircase with pulleys.

That night I felt the *Nautilus* returning to the surface. I heard the small boat going and coming. Then the *Nautilus* plunged again under the waves.

"Where does he take his millions to?" asked Ned Land when I told him.

To that I knew no possible answer.

Our rapid passage across the Mediterranean did not allow Ned Land any opportunity to put his plans into action.

"Do not despair, yet," I told him. "We are off the coast of Portugal. France and England are not far off. There will come a day when we can act with security."

Then one day, "Tonight we shall be but a few miles from the Spanish coast," said Ned. "The opportunity has arrived. Be ready."

I decided to take my notes and nothing more. Then I stationed myself near the door leading to the central staircase and waited for Ned's signal.

At that moment, Captain Nemo appeared.

"I have been looking for you," he said. "Do you know the history of Spain?"

"Very slightly," I answered, wondering what he was driving at.

"In 1702, a great Spanish treasure from America was going to Cadiz. But the Admiral, hearing that an English fleet was cruising these waters, decided to put into Vigo Bay, on the northwest coast of Spain. Unfortunately, before the treasure could be unloaded, the English fleet appeared and a battle followed. Rather than let the treasure fall into enemy hands, every galleon was scuttled, and they

went to the bottom with their immense riches. We are now in Vigo Bay. Follow me!"

I could not refuse.

Through the transparent windows in the saloon, I saw some of the ship's crew in diving clothes. They were clearing ingots of gold and silver, and precious jewels, from half-rotted barrels in blackened shipwrecks.

"Can you understand now the source of the millions I am worth?" said Captain Nemo smiling.

"I understand, sir," I replied. "But I cannot help but think of the unfortunates to whom so much riches, well-distributed, would be of benefit."

"Do you think that these riches are lost because I gather them? Do you think I am ignorant that there are suffering beings and oppressed races on this earth? Do you not understand?"

Captain Nemo stopped, regretting perhaps that he had spoken so much.

But I guessed now for whom those millions were destined. Captain Nemo was still a man, and his heart still beat for humanity. His immense charity was for oppressed races as well as individuals.

"Fortune was against us," I told Ned the next morning.

"Another time we will succeed," said he.

However, Captain Nemo hurried the ship through the Straits of Gibraltar. We were in the Atlantic Ocean. There was no means of escape.

Ned Land was furious.

But I was not particularly sorry, and I returned to my work.

The night of the 19th of February, Captain Nemo paid me an unexpected visit. "You have only visited the submarine depths by daylight. Would you like to see them at night?" he asked.

"Most willingly," I answered.

"You will have far to walk, and must climb a mountain."

"I am ready to follow you."

"Come then, we will put on our diving clothes."

No one else came along. Captain Nemo advanced as if he had often made this trip. I followed my guide who never seemed to tire as we climbed higher and higher.

At the top of the mountain, I looked down the side—into a volcano spewing torrents of lava, but no fire.

Under the lava, ruined, destroyed, lay a town. Its roofs were open to the sky, its temples fallen, its walls sunken, its broad streets deserted.

Where was I?

Captain Nemo picked up a piece of chalk stone. On a black rock he traced one word—

ATLANTIS

I was looking at ruins a thousand generations old.

While I tried to fix every detail in my mind, Captain Nemo remained motionless. What I would have given to know his thoughts, to understand them! The moon gleamed on the buried continent.

Then Captain Nemo signaled, and we returned to the *Nautilus*. We got on board, and the *Nautilus* took off.

The next day I checked the instruments and discovered we were going south. Were we going to the South Pole? No man had ever been there!

Captain Nemo decided to reach the bottom of the ocean. We were now in one of the deepest parts of the Atlantic. The *Nautilus* dived slowly, and its steel plates began to shiver under the great pressure of the water. Outside in the dark waters I saw a few starfish and simple animals. Soon even those disappeared, and all we could see were huge mountains of sleek black stone. Captain Nemo stopped the *Nautilus* and took a photograph of that fantastic landscape. That photograph is still in my possession.

"But we cannot expose the *Nautilus* too long to such great pressure," said Captain Nemo. "Hold on well."

The *Nautilus* shot into the air with great rapidity and emerged into the air like a flying fish. Then it fell, making the waves reach enormous heights.

THE SOUTH POLE

5

We were still going south with great speed. Conseil and I saw icebergs for the first time, and found much to admire. The larger the blocks, the more brilliant the green and copper coloring.

I was warmly dressed and the interior of the *Nautilus* was comfortable. But the wind blew sharply and the icebergs began to appear in greater numbers. It was only a matter of time before they would block our way completely, and one day they did.

"Not only will the *Nautilus* free itself, but it will go further south and reach the South Pole," said Captain Nemo.

"How?" I asked. "Do you intend to give the *Nautilus* wings to fly over these icebergs?"

"No, not *over* them," he said quietly, "but *under* them. There is only one objection. We may not be able to come to the surface for air because of the length of time we have to be under water."

"The *Nautilus* has tanks. We can fill them to supply us with all the oxygen we want," I suggested.

"Another objection is that we may not be able to come to the surface if it is covered with thick ice."

"But the *Nautilus* is armed with a powerful spur!" I reminded him.

"Observe," said Captain Nemo, "that you are now rushing me with arguments in favor of my project."

"Yes, I know that. But the South Pole has not yet been reached by the boldest navigators."

"We will discover it together," said Captain Nemo. "Where others have failed, *I* will not fail."

The *Nautilus* dived to a depth of four hundred fathoms. By degrees, the ice above us became an ice-field, a mountain, a plain. The sea was open, and, at six the next morning we rose, to a world of birds in the air.

"We are at the pole?" I asked.

"I will take our bearings," said Captain Nemo.

A short distance south rose a small island. A boat was launched. Conseil was about to jump onto land when I stopped him.

"Sir," I said to Captain Nemo, "to you belongs the honor of first setting foot on this land."

Captain Nemo jumped lightly onto the sand. He began to take readings, and calculated carefully on his chronometer.

At last, "We are at the South Pole," he said in a grave voice. Then resting his hand on my shoulder, he announced:

"I, Captain Nemo, on this 21st day of March, 1868, have reached the South Pole on the ninetieth degree; and I take possession of this part of the globe, equal to one-sixth of the known continents."

"In whose name, Captain?"

"In my own, sir!"

Captain Nemo unfurled a black banner, bearing an N in gold.

Preparations for departure began the next morning, and by evening the *Nautilus* descended slowly. We were floating under a huge iceberg when a violent shock threw me into the middle of the room. Ned, Conseil and I set out to find Captain Nemo.

"What does it mean?" I asked Captain Nemo when we found him.

"An enormous iceberg, a whole mountain, has turned

over. As it fell, it struck the *Nautilus,* which is now lying on its side."

"Can we right ourselves?"

"Men are working the pumps right now to empty the reservoirs so that the *Nautilus* may regain its balance."

In ten minutes, things hanging in the saloon began to return to their normal positions.

"At last we have righted," I exclaimed.

But as the *Nautilus* rose to the surface, the icebergs around us shifted, closing every outlet. We were imprisoned in a tunnel of ice.

"Unless we can break free, we will suffocate," said Captain Nemo. "We have only two days' supply of air left."

Dressed in diving suits, and working in shifts, the crew attacked the ice at its thinnest point, which was ten feet thick. It would take our pickaxes five nights and four days to set us free, and we had only enough air for two days!

Another problem was also developing. The beds of water around where we worked were freezing fast. Unless something was done we were destined to perish in an ice-tomb, sealed up as in cement.

"I think I have found a solution," said Captain Nemo. "Boiling water!"

"Boiling water?" I cried.

"Yes, jets of boiling water will raise the temperature."

Rapidly, vast machines boiled great quantities of water in the galleys. Powerful pumps forced the water out in great streams. At last the temperature rose to one degree above zero. The danger of freezing was over.

"But we cannot take another day to break through the ice," said Captain Nemo. "There is no air left. We will use the *Nautilus* as a battering ram and break our way through."

Breathing was becoming more and more difficult. My lungs felt as if they were on fire.

"Oh, if I could only not breathe, so as to leave more air for my master," said Conseil.

At that moment, the ice cracked. There was a humming sound under the hull of the *Nautilus*. A panel was opened—almost torn off—and pure air came into all parts of the *Nautilus*.

Just in time to prolong my life, and my gratitude for such devotion from my companion Conseil.

After we rounded Cape Horn, we went northward, and followed the coast of South America at a rapid pace. Where was Captain Nemo taking us? A change had come over him and he shunned us. We had been prisoners on board the *Nautilus* for six months. I wanted to write the true book of the sea. What interesting things I had in my daily notes. Who would believe such animals existed? It was time to think once again of escape!

But there was no opportunity to carry out such a project, and my companions and I were becoming quite disheartened.

I was watching a giant squid through the window of the *Nautilus*. The beast was huge, and seemed irritated by the movements of the boat. Suddenly the *Nautilus* stopped. It was floating, but it did not move.

"What is wrong, sir?" I asked Captain Nemo as he entered the room.

"This monster is entangled in the blades and is preventing our moving. Guns are useless because bullets slide right off its smooth skin. We are going to surface and attack with hatchets."

"And harpoon," said Ned Land, "if you will accept my help."

"I will accept it," said Captain Nemo.

No sooner was the hatch opened when a tentacle slid down the stairway. Captain Nemo cut it with one blow of his axe.

Two more tentacles came down and pulled a seaman up with a powerful suction.

"Help! Help!" cried the seaman in French, which startled me. I had a countryman on board, perhaps several, I

thought while the crew fought to rescue him. They had almost succeeded when the sea monster ejected a stream of black liquid and blinded us. When the liquid disappeared, the squid was gone. So was my unfortunate fellow-countryman. Ten or twelve more squids now invaded the platform and sides of the *Nautilus*, wriggling in waves of blood and ink.

Ned Land plunged his harpoon into their staring eyes, but was suddenly overturned by the tentacles of one he could not avoid. My heart beat with horror as the mouth of the squid opened over him, ready to cut him in two.

I rushed to his aid, but Captain Nemo reached him first, and buried his axe between the two enormous jaws.

Miraculously saved, Ned Land plunged his harpoon deep into the heart of the monster.

"I owed myself this revenge," said Captain Nemo to Ned Land.

Ned Land bowed without replying.

The *Nautilus* was heading north, passing into the Gulf Stream, when Ned Land came to see me.

"I have had enough, I will not stay here. Speak for me, in my name only, if you like," he pleaded.

I sought out Captain Nemo at his desk.

"What is it?" he asked, frowning. "You have interrupted me in an important work. This manuscript contains the sum of my studies of the sea, along with the history of my life. It will be shut up in a case, and the last survivor on board the *Nautilus* will throw it into the sea to be borne to shore by the waves."

"Who knows where the waves will carry it," said I. "I and my companions will keep it for you if you will put us at liberty."

"The answer is no," said Captain Nemo. "Whoever enters the *Nautilus* must never quit it."

"I am willing, like you, to live without liberty," I said, "but it is otherwise with Ned Land."

"The answer is still no."

The sea rose in huge billows. The weather became more and more violent and full of despair, like Captain Nemo. Ned Land isolated himself. All hope of escape faded as hurricanes sent the *Nautilus* beneath the waves.

During the month of May, the weather improved, and the *Nautilus* seemed to be seeking a spot in the water. We were between England and the Scilly Isles when Captain Nemo, on the platform taking the altitude, announced these words—"It is here."

The panels closed, and the *Nautilus* began to sink. Through the window I saw a ruined ship at the bottom of the ocean. The *Nautilus* headed straight for its tomb. Why were we visiting it?

"This vessel belonged to the French Republic," said Captain Nemo. "It fell seventy-four years ago while heroically fighting the English. Its crew of 356 men preferred sinking to surrendering and disappeared under the waves to the cry of 'Long live the Republic!' It was called the *Avenger*! A good name!" said Captain Nemo, crossing his arms.

THE LAST WORDS OF CAPTAIN NEMO

6

It had become clear that it was hatred that had shut Captain Nemo and his companions within the *Nautilus*. But why? What was Captain Nemo's story? What was his nationality? Did his hatred still seek revenge?

I had my answer when we rose to the surface to renew the air, and there was a gunshot from a vessel six miles from us.

"It is a ship of war," said Ned Land.

Seconds later, another explosion hit my ear.

"They are firing on us!" I exclaimed. "Can't they see there are men here?"

We were standing on the platform. A spray of water burst over us from another shell.

"We've got to get out of this!" said Ned Land. "Let's signal! Perhaps they will realize that there are some decent men on board!"

He took out his handkerchief and was about to wave it, when he was struck by the blow of an iron fist and fell on the deck.

"You fool!" cried the Captain. "Do you want me to nail you on the prow of the *Nautilus* before it rams that ship?"

A flood of understanding burst upon me as Captain Nemo unfurled the same black flag he had placed at the North Pole. He *was* using the *Nautilus* for acts of vengeance! It *had* been an engine of destruction on every sea!

41

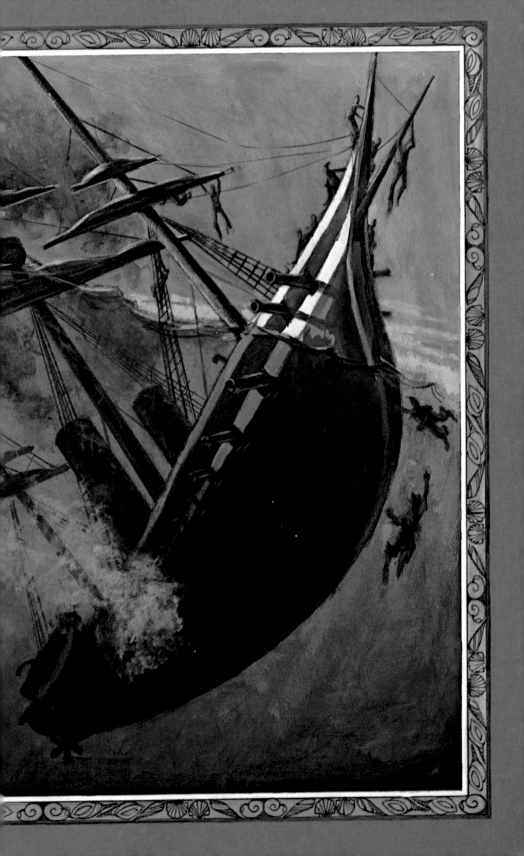

"I advise you not to judge me," he said coldly. "I am the law, and I am the judge! I am the oppressed, and there is the oppressor! Through him I have lost all that I loved—country, wife, children, father and mother. I saw all perish. All that I hate is there!"

Fifteen crewmen joined Captain Nemo and cast looks of hatred at the vessel nearing them.

"Before the *Nautilus* strikes," cried Captain Nemo to the ship of war, "I will lead you away. I would not have your ruins mingle with those below!"

The *Nautilus*, moving with speed, kept just beyond the pursuing ship's guns. Then it submerged and prepared to rush. I felt the power of the steel spur as it passed through the vessel, like a needle through sailcloth!

Ten yards from me, through the viewing windows, I saw the poor crew clinging to the masts, struggling to stay on top of the water.Then they disappeared, and Captain Nemo returned to his room.

Terribly upset, I followed him, and saw on the wall a portrait of a young woman and two little children. Captain Nemo looked at them, stretched his arms towards them, and kneeling down burst into deep sobs.

But I felt only horror for Captain Nemo. Whatever he had suffered at the hands of men, he had no right to punish them.

After this episode, the *Nautilus* was always under water, and it was difficult to know where we were going. Then one night, Ned Land woke me.

"I have discovered we are in sight of land. We are going to try to escape."

We set the escape time for ten o'clock. How long that day seemed! I remained alone. At six o'clock I ate dinner, though I was not hungry. Then I went into the saloon to check the direction of the *Nautilus*. We were heading north at a great speed.

I took one last look at all those wonders of nature and art treasures in the museum. I wanted it all to be fixed in my mind forever. Then I returned to my room. My heart was beating fast and I found it impossible to keep cool. I controlled a strong impulse to walk into the Captain's room and have it out with him.

I lay down and tried to relax. I thought back over all our adventures: the *Abraham Lincoln*, Atlantis, the ice shelf, the fight with the squids, and more. Among these events Captain Nemo stood out in my mind as a giant. He was no longer my equal, but the king of the seas!

I dressed myself in sea-clothing and collected my notes. Then I crept along the dark stairs of the *Nautilus,* reached the door of the saloon, and opened it gently.

Captain Nemo was playing the organ.

Avoiding the slightest sound, I was going to open the door to the library when a sigh from Captain Nemo nailed me to the spot. As he came toward me, he was sobbing, and murmured these words (the last which ever struck my ear)—

"Almighty God! Enough! Enough!"

Was it a confession of remorse from this man's conscience?

I rushed through the library, mounted the staircase, and joined Ned and Conseil who were loosening the bolts to the small boat.

"Let us go!" I cried.

Just then we heard voices nearby. But it was not we the crew were looking for.

"The maelstrom! The maelstrom!" they cried.

We were on the dangerous coast of Norway. Pent-up waters between the islands of Ferros and Lofoten rushed with irresistible violence, forming a whirlpool from which no vessel ever escaped.

What a situation to be in!

"We must hold on," said Ned. "We may still be saved if we stick—"

In the middle of his words we heard a crashing noise. Our small boat was hurled like a stone from a sling into the midst of the whirlpool. My head struck on a piece of iron, and I lost all consciousness.

How the boat escaped from the whirlpool—how Ned Land, Conseil and myself ever came out of it, I cannot tell. But we embraced each other heartily when we awoke in a fisherman's hut on the coast of Norway.

While I am waiting for a steamboat which will take me to France, I am working on my adventures once more.

Will the world believe me? I do not know. In less than ten months, I covered twenty thousand leagues, and saw the wonders of seven seas.

What happened to the *Nautilus*? Does Captain Nemo still live? Shall we ever know what his real name was, or his real nationality? Will the waves one day wash up on shore his manuscript, holding the story of his life?

I hope so. If he still lives, may the judge disappear, and the scientist continue the peaceful exploration of the sea!

GLOSSARY

conscience (kän′ chəns)   a feeling about the rightness or wrongness of one's own acts

harpoon (här pōōn′)   A spear that is used for hunting whales and other sea animals

maelstrom (māl′ strəm)   a strong whirlpool that can suck objects into its center

narwhal (när′ hwäl′)   a large Arctic sea animal which in the male has a long ivory tusk

navigate (nav′ə gāt′)   to travel and find one's way in a ship

oppress (ə pres′)   to rule or control cruelly

shipwreck (ship′ rek′)   A ruined and sunken ship

squid (skwid)   a sea animal related to the octopus that has a long body and ten arms

submarine (səb′ mə rēn′)   a boat that can travel under the surface of the water

suffocate (səf′ ə kat′)   to die because of a lack of air